Killing

with

Candy

A FIFO WIVES 'SWEET DELIGHTS' NOVELETTE

Dragonfly Publishing

LISA WOLSTENHOLME

Copyright

Published by Dragonfly Publishing, May 2022

© Lisa Wolstenholme.

A catalogue record for this work is available from the National Library of Australia

ISBN(sc): 978-0-6454370-5-8

ISBN (e): 978-0-6454370-6-5

*"Loving someone liberates the lover as well as the beloved,
and that kind of love comes with age."*

- Maya Angelou

S tella was pissed off. Her husband Dave, a FIFO engineer, had just returned to Tom Price Mine in the Pilbara and she was once again left to manage the house, the kids and the cat—Miss Pink Fluffy Bum—alone.

Dave worked eight days on, four days off leaving little time for leisure *or* pleasure. Stella had become accustomed to his excuses of tiredness and lack of energy when it came to day-to-day activities; he worked hard to support his family of four, but she was increasingly frustrated by the lack of romance and night-time antics between them.

Dave was also hell-bent on squirreling money away for a 'rainy' day with little left for fun and frolics. Dave was on a good salary but was a complete and utter scrooge. They hadn't had a holiday for over two years.

A Skype with Dave later that evening soon turned Stella's mood from mildly unsavoury to downright sour as Mr Grumps fired off a string of questions: "Did you sort out Dillon's soccer money?" and "Did you get Poppy some new shoes?" then "We've only got fifty bucks left in the chequing account—what the hell have you been spending money on?"

Stella's shoulders slumped. No, she hadn't sorted the soccer money out or bought Poppy new shoes—there was bugger-all money to do that with once the bills had been paid, the kids' needs met and groceries bought.

"I'm sorry, Dave. I guess I lost track."

"Sorry's not gonna pay for a roof over your head and put food on the table until my next pay packet, is it?"

Stella was usually careful with money so resented Dave's Question Time, but the truth was desperation had set in when it became clear her and Dave's love life was on permanent simmer. She found herself taking comfort in a cheeky bottle or two of wine to escape her humdrum existence and dreaming of times when her sex life was most definitely on a rolling boil.

"I could try and get a job?"

"And who would look after the kids when I'm not there?"

Stella shook her head, her eyes welling up with tears. "We could use some of our savings?"

Dave scowled. "We are NOT touching our savings. How many times have we gone over this?"

"But Dave… we haven't gone overboard with money. Don't you think it's time we treated ourselves?"

Stella gave him her best 'sad puppy' eyes but he just rolled his.

The next afternoon, Stella sat outside Poppy's classroom waiting for her school-mum pals, Jess and Nina, to arrive.

"What's up, Stell? You look like you've been told Michael Fassbender's gay," Jess said as she plopped down next to her friend.

"Dave," Stella said glumly.

"What's he done now?"

"Getting shitty about money… again."

"For eff's sake. He doesn't change much, does he?"

"What's Grumps done?" Nina said, bounding up to the two women.

"The usual," Stella said with a sigh.

"Bloody hell, does he ever let up?"

"You know Dave. Likes to stash his cash under the mattress. Anyone would think he was 80 not 38!"

"Shame he doesn't do anything else where the mattress is concerned," Jess scoffed.

The three women "tsk'd" in unison.

"Men, honestly," Nina said, rolling her eyes. "Can't live with 'em, can't live without 'em."

"I'm guessing you didn't get any of the sweet stuff during his last stopover?" Jess said, shaking her head.

"What do you think?"

"I think we're *all* still waiting for the monsoon to arrive to quench our arid deserts!"

The three women belly-laughed, united in their lack of bedroom action.

Eight-year-old Poppy came bounding out of the classroom over to her mum.

"Guess what!" she announced, holding up a piece of card.

"What, Popsicle?"

"I got another reading award!" She pushed the certificate under Stella's nose.

"Well aren't you the clever one!" Stella pulled her daughter close and gave her a squeeze, her proud-parent face beaming.

"Hey Mum," Jess's son, Zak, called as he whizzed past his mum and over to the monkey bars to play with his mates.

"I'm guessing Zak didn't get an award," Jess said, "unless you count reading comics!" She let out a giggle and congratulated Poppy.

"Muummmm," Poppy said with a whine. "My feet hurt!" She looked down at her shoes. "My toes are all squishy."

"It's okay, darling. We'll buy you some more shoes when Daddy gets paid." Stella glanced over at Nina, who just rolled her eyes.

"Okay," Poppy said as Nina's daughter, Pearl, approached. The two girls linked arms and skipped over to the playground—their usual school pick-up routine knowing full well their mums wouldn't be done chatting for at least another ten minutes.

"Right, I'd better round up my boy and get him to cricket practice," Jess said. She gave her friends a quick peck on the cheek and set off to find her son, now nowhere to be seen.

"Damn!" Stella clasped her cheeks as she bolted upright.

"What's the matter?' Nina said.

"Dillon's soccer money. His teacher asked for it two weeks ago, but I don't have any spare cash until Dave gets paid."

"I can lend you it. How much?"

Stella hated borrowing money and this wasn't the first time her friends had bailed her out, but what else could she do? Dillon would be gutted if he was thrown off the team because his subs hadn't been paid. "Twenty bucks," Stella said glumly.

Nina fished around in her bag and took out her purse, clicking it open and handing Stella two $10 notes.

"Thanks, Nina. You're a life saver."

"You'd do the same."

"You sure about that? Mr Grumps wouldn't loosen the purse strings enough for me to be able to!"

"Ain't that the truth," Nina said, tittering.

Stella said her goodbyes, called Poppy over and the two walked towards Dillon's classroom.

Dillon was slumped on the bag bench outside the classroom as Stella and Poppy approached.

"Dill? You okay?"

"Mr Haynes said I can't do soccer anymore because you haven't paid my subs." Dillon's eyes glistened.

"Wait here, Popsicle. I need to have a word with Dill's teacher," she said to Poppy, then turned to her distraught son. "I'll sort it out, Dill. Don't worry."

Stella headed into the classroom filled with low grey melamine tables and hobbit-sized chairs and may her way to Mr Haynes' desk. Before the stony-faced teacher could get a word out Stella blurted, "I'm so sorry this is so late. We've had some money issues of late, but here's Dillon's soccer money." She placed the money on the desk, pushed it towards him and waited, staring down at her feet like a naughty child.

"On time in future, please," he said with a growl.

Stella was busy prepping dinner when Poppy came in with her usual 5 pm question: "Muuummm. What's for dinnerrrrr?"

"Roast chook and veggies," Stella said, chopping up sweet potatoes.

"Yuck!" Poppy scrunched her face. "I hate veggies." She tilted her chin up, performed her best prissy princess pirouette and stomped out of the kitchen.

Stella could hear her whinging to Dillon about having to eat, "the same yucky stuff EVERY DAY," and shook her head.

Bloody Dave!

After dinner was finished and the kids had been showered, put to bed and read to—which could take anywhere between one and three hours depending on who took the longest to eat their cold veggies that had been sitting on the plate for over 45 minutes, or who whinged about going in the shower the most, or who took the longest to *find* their toothbrush, or which story had to be read three times in a row for the child to be satisfied enough to go to sleep—Stella sat in an exhausted heap on the sofa and pulled out her laptop to Skype Dave. Admittedly, she wasn't feeling that enthusiastic about it, mainly because Skyping, like their lives in general, had become somewhat of a forced routine with questions like, "What kind of a day have you had?" and "Have the kids had a good day at school?" and "Where have you been today?" and usually ending with, "How much money have you spent?" courtesy of Mr Grumps.

Stella was tired of it all and often found herself daydreaming of what life would be like if Dave wasn't around at all. She would get a job in PR again, make decent money and put the kids in afterschool care until she got home. They'd live in a modern three by two in a nicer suburb near school and spend the weekends going out on adventures in the bush, bike riding, crafting, baking and going to the cinema. They'd go on family holidays every school break and every so often, she'd go out with Jess and Nina, get steaming drunk and talk about why life is so much easier without a man around. But then the guilt would soon creep in and she'd remember all the love and support Dave had given her over the years, how she could be a mum and not have to think about returning to work, and how he used to be before becoming a FIFO worker when weekends *were* for family time, and action in the bedroom was regularly on the menu. It wasn't Dave's fault he was made redundant from his 9 to 5 desk job. FIFO work in the mines became the best solution after they'd just bought a bigger house with an even bigger home loan repayment, and he worked so hard it was no wonder he was knackered when he returned home. Stella couldn't begrudge him much-needed rest and recuperation, could she? And to be fair, he wasn't always a grump; he could be fun, flirtatious and full of life, and an absolute stallion in the sack!

But still... life without having to answer to anyone and accounting for every cent spent? Sweet dreams, for sure.

Stella pushed the thoughts back into the dark

recesses of her mind and clicked on Dave's name to start the Skype call.

He answered straightaway, and with a beaming grin launched into his usual, "Hey Stell." The calm before the storm.

Stella forced a smile. "Good day, love?"

"The usual. How was yours?"

"Yeah… the usual." No point pretending it was anything but the same-old, same-old. No reason to tell him life was amazing when it was so far removed from 'amazing', Stella could have been on Mars.

"Great. Did you sort out Dill's soccer money?"

Stella's chest tightened. *Here we go…*

It was a school night, but after the call with Dave, Stella wanted nothing more than to sit on the sofa watching re-runs of "Married at First Sight" while drinking several glasses of Cab Sav. She watched dumbfounded as mis-matched couples pulled out all the stops to try and make a faux marriage work or spend the entire time doing their best to piss each other off, something she and Dave had become quite adept at.

Watching other people's sham marriages helped take her mind off Dave's last comment on the call about sending the kids to a state school or changing the car to a cheaper model to save money. Stella knew full well there was a sizeable amount of cash sitting in their savings account gathering gold dust. Dave was being unreasonable, wasn't he? What was 'rainy day' money for, anyway? They weren't saving for a new house, their mortgage was being comfortably paid off, and the car had no finance on it because Dave didn't believe in credit. What was the point of having money stashed away when it could be used *now* to improve the quality of all their lives? But in the back of her mind, Stella knew why–Dave was paranoid about being made redundant again and wanted to ensure they had money available if needed. It *did* make sense, but it also seemed that really living and enjoying life was permanently on hold and it frustrated Stella, which led to resentment, which in turn led to the daydreams of a life without Dave in it.

Oh crap. Has it really got to this?

Stella already knew the answer but felt completely

stuck for what to do about it. She was secretly envious of the faux marriages on the TV that appeared to be working because the couple seemed to genuinely like each other and love was brewing.

Something had to give.

Stella was fed up with the way her life was playing out and the time for action had arrived. In a moment of clarity, she picked up her mobile and texted Jess.

Dave's doing my head in and I don't know what to do. Help!

She took a glug of wine and waited for Jess's reply, which came moments later.

Just bump him off ;-)

Quickly followed by,

I know a guy

Stella gasped. *She's not serious, is she?*

I hope you're joking!

Maybe ;-)

I'm being serious, J. Me and Dave are going staler than three-day-old bread!

Stella drummed her fingers on her wine glass as she waited for Jess to reply.

You and Dave need some sexy time

That's your answer to everything!

Because it works. A man will give you anything you want after he's just had a blow job!

Typical! Well, I'm not feeling very sexy at the moment

I should hope not, you're texting me!

Stella erupted into a fit of giggles as she read the text, realising Jess had a point—she couldn't remember the last time she and Dave had had sex, but was damn sure it was something she *could* change. It would either kill or cure them.

The next day at school pickup and still nursing a sore head from drinking nearly two bottles of wine the night before, Stella waited anxiously for her friends to arrive; she had a plan of attack and needed their help.

"Gather round, ladies," she said as Nina and Jess arrived. She glanced around to make sure no one was in hearing distance as she beckoned them closer. "I'm thinking of trying to entice Dave into some sexy talk over Skype. You know… start with a few hints here and there, then on Tuesday night before he flies back, I'll up the ante, so by the time he gets home he is so up for it he'll jump my bones the minute we get in the door."

Jess pulled back, a smirk crossing her face. "You think he'll go for it?"

"I hope so, it's just… well, I've never really done anything like that before."

"Really? Not even before Dave?" Nina said, her voice raising an octave.

"No, never and I don't really know where to start."

"Don't worry, Stell, me and Nina can help you out with this one, can't we Nina?" Jess shoved shoulders with the other woman and tossed her a wink.

Stella wasn't sure if she was excited or *terrified* by the prospect.

That Saturday evening, and with Dillon, Zak, Poppy and Pearl all outside running riot in the yard, Stella, Jess and Nina sat around Stella's kitchen bench, wine in hand, ready to help Stella plan out Skype-Gate.

"So how do I get this started?" Stella said,

grabbing a pen and notepad and waiting for the pearls of wisdom she hoped would come from her two friends.

"Hmmm… well, since you're a Skype-sex virgin, perhaps we need to start with the basics," Nina said.

"And what are they?"

Nina and Jess looked at each other, both smirking, and in unison said, "Boobs!"

"What about them?" Stella was puzzled.

Nina downed some wine, placed it back on the counter and leaned in towards Stella. "They're your best asset when it comes to lighting the flames of desire with your man, unless you're willing to stick a rocket up his butt!" She fell about laughing, Jess quickly joining in.

"What am I supposed to do with them?"

"Christ, Stell! It's a wonder you have kids," Jess said leaning forward and gesturing as though her boobs were falling out. "Get those puppies out!"

"What? Just pop 'em out mid-conversation?"

"No, you idiot." Jess clasped her cheeks, shaking her head in dismay. "When you Skype Dave, make sure you have a nice dressing gown or tunic on and nothing underneath. Then, when Dave's droning on about whatever it is he goes on about, pull back the top part just a little so that a smidge of boobage is visible, and see how he reacts."

"But what about the kids? What if they come in while I'm... exposing myself?"

"You're not exposing them, just a smidge. Enough to give Dave a teaser of what's to come. Just make sure the kids are fast asleep in bed before you start."

Stella paused, rubbing her chin as she contemplated this advice. "Then what?" she finally said.

Nina let out a belly-laugh. "Jeez, Stell. Don't you remember anything about foreplay?" and shook her head.

"Of course I do, but it's hardly foreplay if he's not actually there with me, is it?"

Jess sighed and topped up her wine. "That's the point! You're building him up so he's ready to ravage your bones by the time he gets home, not sealing the deal right there and then!"

"Fine. So what then?"

"Well, if he gets distracted by the boobage, you wait a little while and then 'accidentally' show a little bit more."

"Accidentally?"

"I'm gonna need more wine for this," Nina said huffing, and strolled around the counter to Stella's fridge to hunt down another bottle.

"Jess?" Stella said. "Do you agree with this?"

"Abso-bloody-lutely! I used to do it with Kev when he was away on business. It's easy!"

"Maybe for you."

"Just give it a go and see what happens."

"But I'll feel... ridiculous."

"Maybe at first, but you'll get the hang of it."

Nina plopped the now open bottle of vino on the counter next to Stella and Jess. "Top-up ladies. We're in for a long night."

Stella poured more wine into her glass and held her pen over the pad. "Right. Hit me up with more suggestions, gals. I'm making a list."

"Well, for starters, make sure 'drink copious amounts of wine to loosen me up' is top of that list!" Nina said, stifling a snort.

"Very funny."

"I'm not joking, Stell. If you're gonna do this, you need to stop being so uptight. If Janet Jackson can get away with flashing a boob on stage in front of thousands then so can you in the privacy of your own home. It's not like he's never seen them before. He has seen them before, hasn't he? You're not some kind of prude, are you?"

Stella shot a death stare at Nina.

It was after eleven pm when the kids were finally tiring and Jess and Nina had called Ubers to take them all home.

After the goodbyes were said and Poppy and Dillan were safely stashed in their beds, Stella slinked down onto the sofa and scrutinised her list, her eyes falling on number five:

'Re-enact the scene in Basic Instinct where Sharon Stone uncrosses her legs.'

What the fuck?

Stella's finger hovered over the mouse pointer. The

kids had been in bed for over an hour, she'd already drunk two glasses of Cab Sav in the space of forty minutes and was wearing her pink satin dressing gown with only black lacy knickers underneath. But her heart was beating faster than a heavy metal drummer and she dare not press the 'call' button for fear that Dave would either not respond to her sexgestions or would respond way too much and the call would get messy.

It took several more gulps of wine and many deep breaths before she plucked up enough courage to do the deed.

The familiar DUR-DE-DUURR tone rang out and she bolted to the strategically placed armchair several feet away from the laptop sitting on her bed.

"Hi love." Dave's dulcet tones resounded.

Stella smoothed over her gown and tried to focus on her husband, the two-and-a-bit glasses of wine having already taken effect.

"Hi Dave. How was your day?" she said in a lowered tone hoping to sound more Lauren Bacall and less Kath & Kim.

"Why are you so far away from the screen?" he

said, leaning towards his webcam.

"Thought I'd change it up a bit," Stella replied, gently twirling her wine glass to further emphasise her sultry pose.

"I can barely hear you. You need to come closer."

"Hang on. I'll up the volume," Stella said, trying her best to rise from the chair without the gown gaping open. But it wasn't the getting up and walking towards the laptop that was to be her undoing. As she bent to increase the volume, she suddenly noticed her image on the upper right-hand part of the screen, and she was showing far more boobage than was intended.

"Whoa! Stell, what are you doing?" Dave said as her exposed breasts rested on the keyboard like two large scoops of ice cream on a platter.

"Crap!" Stella hurriedly pulled the gown tightly across her chest and darted back to the chair.

"Have you just got out of the shower or something?"

"Um… yeah. Sorry about that." Stella's cheeks flushed. But soon her embarrassment turned to annoyance. Dave had been privy to a face-full of boobs and all he wanted to know was if she'd had a shower.

What the fuck's wrong with him?

It didn't take long for Dave to launch into his usual interrogation and between questions, Stella either gave her stock answer, sighed or took another sip of wine, all thoughts of a remote seduction cast aside along with her dignity.

"Well?" Jess said, arms folded and eyes wide.

"It was a nightmare. Don't know why I bothered."

"Why? What happened?"

"He couldn't hear me properly because I was sitting too far away, so I went to up the volume and accidentally flashed *all* my boobs in the process."

"Did it work?"

"Did it hell! He wanted to know if I'd just got out of the shower!" Stella said, tutting. "He didn't say a thing about the puppies."

"No reaction at all?"

"Nope."

A wry smile crossed Jess's face. "You need to up

your game. It's time to invoke item 5 on the list."

Stella stared in shock. "Tell me you're kidding? The boobs were supposed to work and didn't."

"Don't you worry about that. I defy any straight guy to not get a hard-on at the flash of a pussy."

Stella paused to ponder. It had been so long since Dave had shown any interest in her nether regions that she wondered if he would even recognise them. "Do you think I should get my foofoo waxed? She's a bit unkempt."

Jess curled up with laughter and Stella's face dropped, an expression that could sour the ripest of fruit.

"Wax away if it makes you feel sexy," Jess said between giggles, her face turning the colour of Stella's dressing gown from the night before.

"You're not helping, you know!" Stella turned away from her friend as annoyance gripped. All she wanted was a few tips and tricks to help her get Dave fired up but ended up feeling as though she were about to star in a really bad porno. Less *Debbie Does Dallas* and more *Stella Stops Sexing*.

"Lighten up, Stell," Jess said. "You need more

wine before the next attempt."

"I'm going to end up an alcy at this rate. And for what?" Stella huffed. "How many women do you know who've turned to alcohol to improve their sex lives?"

"At least two," Jess replied. "Me and you."

It was Monday, and two days before Dave returned home. Jess and Nina had somehow managed to convince Stella to give Skype-Gate another go, ignoring her protests and plying her with several bottles of red wine.

By the time the kids were in bed and Stella had called both Nina and Jess for moral support, *and* downed nearly a full bottle of Merlot, she was determined to give it one last-ditch attempt.

It's now or never.

As before, she set the laptop up on the bed and positioned the armchair a good foot-or-so away. She made sure the volume was on max *before* the call and once again donned the dressing gown, sans underwear. She was resolute; item five on her 'How to Seduce Dave' list was going to be enacted that night.

Everything was now in place and Stella once again hovered her finger over the mouse pointer.

I can do this. I CAN do this.

She took a long glug of wine and clicked.

DUR-DE-DUURR

DUR-DE-DUURR

DUR-DE-DUURR

Where the fuck is he?

DUR-DE-DUURR

The BWOOP sound finally came and Dave's face appeared on the laptop screen. His brown, lightly curled hair was messy and his face was pale.

"Dave? You okay?"

"Yeah… long day, love," Dave said, running his hand through his dishevelled mane.

"You look stressed."

"It's nothing. Like I said–long day."

"Do you want to talk about it?" Stella said, brows furrowed with concern for her husband.

"Nah," he replied, then changed the subject. "How's your day been?"

"Okay."

"You showered again? Seems to be a regular thing now."

For a moment, Stella could swear he glanced up and down her body as she sat cross-legged in the armchair, wine glass in hand. It caused a tingle in her nether regions. Resolved to making Skype-Gate work, she tilted her head, half-smiled and said in a soft, low tone, "I want to be fresh for you."

Dave's eyes widened and his full lips curled upwards.

Bingo!

It was now or never. She'd got his full attention and her next manoeuvre would hopefully cause something else to become full.

In slow motion, she uncrossed her legs. Dave's eyes widened like full moons, and Stella's heart thumped so loud she thought it might jump out of her chest and perform a conga around the bedroom.

"Stella..." Dave said, his voice like molten whiskey.

The moment of reveal was just about to happen when the bedroom door creaked open and Miss Pink Fluffy Bum walked in and jumped on Stella's lap.

"Argh!" Stella bolted upright, quickly followed by her shouting, "That fucking cat!" Her glass of wine toppled and fell to the floor, spraying the beige bedroom carpet with red wine.

She ignored the fact that Dave was unbuttoning his pants and scrambled to shove the mischievous moggy out of the bedroom and head off to the kitchen to find something to get the wine stain out of the carpet, all thoughts of seduction now in a land far, far away.

Where's the fucking salt and rice?

Stella didn't know whether to laugh or cry as she recounted the previous night's events to Jess and Nina. It seemed to her that the Universe was conspiring against them when it came to igniting the flames of desire, and Jess and Nina were not helping in the slightest, judging by the guffaws coming out of them.

"That's it. I'm giving up and buying a vibrator," Stella said, turning away from her friends in disgust.

"Works for me," Nina said, still clutching her

sides as laughter resounded.

But in a moment of reflection, Jess turned to Stella and said, "At least give it one more try. Everything that's happened so far has been out of your control."

"I guess. But will it ever be in my control? Maybe the Universe is telling me Dave and I are well-and-truly passed the sexy times and we should settle for being Mr and Mrs Comfy-Slippers."

"That's bollocks," Nina said, her face contorted as if she'd just swallowed a fly. "You're taking the easy way out." She scowled at Stella.

"No I'm not. I'm just being real. No point flogging a dead horse."

"Maybe it's Dave you should be flogging!" Jess said, giggling like a schoolgirl who'd just seen a willy for the first time.

"Jess! This is serious." Stella's mood was dropping lower than an underground train, and at a similar speed, too.

Jess and Nina looked at each other, their faces contorted as they tried to hold in the sniggers.

"Okay, maybe we need to re-examine the list,"

Nina offered, tilting her head to the side.

"I'm done with the bloody list." Stella folded her arms and pursed her lips. "It's done bugger-all for my sex life so far."

"C'mon, Stell. Let's give it one more go. I'm sure between the three of us we can come up with a foolproof way of getting you and Dave back on the road to bliss."

Stella suspected Nina and Jess were not taking her dilemma as seriously as she wanted but admitted defeat and nodded her agreement.

"My place at seven. I'll get some wine on my way home," Nina said, a wry smile crossing her face.

Stella hurried the kids into the car, her mind spinning with ideas for Dave's online seduction, but was it futile? He'd be home in a few days, anyway, so maybe she should focus on a home-based sexy soiree?

As the car pulled up in the driveway and Stella turned off the engine, Poppy leaned across to her mum from the back seat.

"Muuumm?"

"Yes, Popsicle?"

Poppy fished around in her pocket, pulled out a piece of paper and started to read it. "What is boobage and why do you want to show Daddy a foofoo?"

Stella let out an involuntary gasp.

OH my God!

"Poppy… what have you got there?" she said, trying to keep her tone even.

"This! I found it on the kitchen table." Poppy thrust the paper towards Stella. Stella grabbed it with lightning speed and looked down at her familiar handwriting.

How the hell I am going to explain this?

"Oh… Popsicle… erm…" Stella squirmed. "This is just something silly Mummy was writing. It's not for you to worry about."

That should do it.

"But what *is* boobage?" Poppy was persistent.

Quick as a flash, Stella replied, "I'll tell you when you're older."

"Okay," Poppy said and rushed out of the car.

Stella's hands trembled as she held the paper with

the list of 'How to seduce Dave on Skype'. Her eyes scanned over the items:

1. *Wear only a bathrobe on the call and accidentally flash boobage, then accidentally expose more as the call goes on.*

2. *Send Dave a "sext" while he's on the call and encourage him to talk dirty to me.*

3. *Reminisce over sexier times we've had in the past.*

4. *Ask Dave to role-play being a repair man and tell him he needs to check my plumbing and describe how he's going to do it.*

5. *Re-enact the scene in 'Basic Instinct' where Sharon Stone uncrosses her legs and shows her foofoo while being questioned by the police (make sure foofoo is presentable before showing Dave).*

6. *Ask Dave what he'd like to do in the sack when he gets home (and not just sleep).*

7. *If none of these work, just give up and join an effing Nunnery.*

Stella didn't know whether to laugh or cry at the thought of Poppy reading the list. Would she be mentally scarred by its contents? Would she know what Stella was intending to do? She shook her head at the thought, scrunched the paper up and threw it in the car bin bag, then retrieved it when she remembered her and the girls would be reviewing it later.

This is crazy. What the hell was I thinking agreeing to this?

After dinner, Stella bundled the kids back into the car and drove off to Nina's house, all the while trying to act as if nothing untoward had happened—what with Poppy finding the list. Her nerves were shot, her pulse still zooming with either dread or excitement, she wasn't sure which.

When the trio arrived at Nina's, Stella was out of the car and sitting at the kitchen table with a glass of red quicker than a cheetah chasing a gazelle.

"God, I need this," she said with a sigh and took another glug.

"You alright, Stell?" Nina asked, topping up Stella's glass.

"Not really. Poppy found the damn list!"

Nina tossed her head backwards and let out a series of cackles. "Oh my God! What did she do?"

"It's not so much what she did, it was what she said!" Stella said, her voice raising five octaves as she bolted upright. "She asked me what 'boobage' was and why I wanted to show her dad my foofoo."

By this point, Nina was doubled-up as belly-laughs poured out of her.

Jess arrived and asked what had happened.

Nina, now with tears streaming down her cheeks, tried to get the words out, but was laughing too much.

Stella's face turned to stone as she passed the list to Jess. "Poppy found this and wanted to know about my pussy and boobage."

Jess read the list and spluttered, "Have they had their sex-ed class at school yet?" before bursting into fits of giggles.

Nina managed to stop laughing enough to pour Jess a glass of wine while Stella guzzled hers. She was going to need more than Dutch Courage to get through this night.

Once the girls had calmed down and the kids were occupied playing games in Pearl's bedroom, Stella decided the time had come to review the dreaded list and come up with a hundred percent sure-fire way of re-igniting Dave's flames of desire.

She picked up the list lying on the table in front of Jess and cleared her throat. "Ladies, we have work to do."

Nina and Jess looked at each other and grinned.

Stella took out her pen and struck items one and five from the list.

"Well?" she said, glaring across at Jess and Nina and waiting for them to share their ideas.

"I got nothing," Nina said first.

Jess shrugged her shoulders. "I dunno. Dave's a tough gig." She sipped her wine as if to distract attention.

"Oh come on! You two got me into this, now tell me how to get Dave into me!" Stella banged her fist on the table as desperation gripped, the two other women raising their eyebrows in unison at her.

"Look, Stell, I'm not sure what more we can suggest," Nina said with a frown. "Perhaps trying to get Dave going over Skype is a bad idea."

"But—"

"Yeah… maybe just wait until he gets home,"

Jess said, shrugging again.

"Fat lot of help you two are!" Stella said, huffing her annoyance. "The whole idea was to get him fired up so he'd jump my bones as soon as he got back."

"Well, it's clearly not been working, so maybe we should just cut our losses and move on."

"Nina! I'm not some kind of investment, you know."

"Okay, okay. Maybe we're going about this the wrong way."

"I'll say."

Jess butted in, "Nina, what about that game you bought a few years back. You know, the one you used to get Josh's appetite whetted?"

Nina smirked. "Oh yeah… the Ann Summer's Board Game. Worked a treat." Her eyes rolled to the side as if she were reminiscing raunchier times with her hubby.

"What?" Stella said with a start. "You never mentioned this game before. Have you still got it?"

"I think so. Probably stashed at the back of my closet so Pearl never finds it."

Stella was reminded of Poppy's earlier

questioning about the list.

"Can you find it? Like, now?" Jess said.

"Well... okay. Give me a few minutes."

As Nina trotted off to find the game, Stella said to Jess, "And have *you* got any games that I should know about?"

"Um... not ones that I'm willing to share," she replied, smirking.

"Bloody typical," Stella said sarcastically.

Nina returned several minutes later, slightly out of breath but holding a box in her hand. "Found it!" she said with glee.

She put it on the table, blew off the thick layer of dust on top and prised the lid off.

"This, ladies, is the answer to everything."

The kids were fed, watered, read to and *hopefully* asleep in bed.

Stella had showered, tidied up her foofoo, shaved everything that shouldn't be hairy, and donned only her satin pink dressing gown. The board game was open and on the bed, the laptop perched next to it, and Stella laid on her side facing the screen with a soupcon of cleavage on show.

The customary glass of wine sat on her bedside table. She rolled across the bed to grab it and take a sip, but accidentally knocked the side of the board causing the cards and game pieces to slide off.

Great start, Stella!

After having more than a sip and putting the game pieces back into place, she took a long breath and with trembling fingers, opened Skype on her laptop.

The familiar sounds rang out until Dave finally answered the call.

"Hi love, sorry but I can't stay on long. There's been a problem at the site and I'm needed there."

"Dave…" Stella said with a whinge. "But I had something special planned."

"You could call me back later?" Dave suggested.

"What time will you be finished? It's already after nine."

"I don't know. Depends on what the problem is."

Stella let out an audible sigh. "Will you text me when you're done?"

"If it's not too late… So what's the surprise?"

"Well, there's no point in telling you now, is there?"

"Don't be like that, Stell. I gotta go when I'm called. You know the drill."

She sighed again, this time knowing full well that there was nothing she could do about it; Dave had to do what he needed to do.

"I'm sorry. I'm just disappointed, I guess."

"I'll be home soon. Can it wait until then?"

"It'll have to," Stella replied, her mood nose-diving.

"Talk soon," Dave said, faux-smiling as if knowing that Stella was gutted.

"Yeah... bye, love."

The call ended and Stella packed away the laptop and game, drank the remainder of wine, snuggled into bed and drifted off to sleep.

She was briefly woken by a ping from her phone, but instead of checking it, fell back into slumber.

The next morning, she noticed the text notification on her phone.

"Shit!" she said out loud after reading it. Dave had returned at around ten-thirty and was hoping to receive his surprise only, Stella was deep in slumber and completely missed it.

My last chance at starting up the engine and I bloody missed it!

The following day, after hearing about the lack of game-play the night before and Stella completely missing round two, Jess suggested they needed some retail therapy.

Nina wasn't able to join them; she was attending a High School Open Day, so it was down to Jess to cheer up the now deflated Stella.

The two friends dropped their kids off at school and went in Jess's car to the Mayfields Gate shopping complex.

Stella was not in a happy place as they hit the shops. She was preoccupied with going through the list of things needing doing before Dave arrived home. The house needed cleaning, the washing was stacking up in the laundry, and she was running low on groceries; all the things that would annoy Dave when he returned and ensure he would be in no mood for *any* kind of sweet loving.

"Have you got the list?" Jess's question came out-of-the-blue.

"No. Why?"

"Because Dave's coming home tonight. Don't you need to prepare?"

"Prepare for what? It's all been a farce so far."

"Oh don't be a sour puss. I thought you wanted to get Dave all hot-and-bothered?"

"I do… I mean, I *did*. Don't know if I can be bothered now. Besides, I've got a mountain of things to do before he gets back."

"So you're just gonna give up?"

"I guess I am."

"Not on my watch, baby." Jess's eyes narrowed and a wry smile crossed her face.

"Jess? What are you planning?" Stella glared at her friend, her suspicions roused.

"Well, I just thought that since we're here, we might as well invest in some nice, new, possibly quite sexy clothes."

"Oh right. Is that what you thought." Stella said, tutting.

"Who doesn't need to refresh their underwear

collection once in a while?" Jess fluttered her eyelashes and gave Stella a saccharine grin.

"Dave won't like it if I spend too much money," Stella replied in a deadpan tone.

"Then we'll just get one set. Dave won't mind, especially if it's—you know—nice to look at."

Why do I let her talk me into things like this?

"Fine. Just one set."

"Well c'mon then. Let's go and find something shecksy for you to dazzle Dave with."

Defeated, Stella rolled her eyes, shook her head and trudged along beside Jess.

Stella picked up the white lacy bra she'd spied in Target, holding it aloft for Jess to inspect. "This one?"

"It's a bit virtuous," Jess said, scrunching her nose. "You're thirty-two not seventeen. You want it to scream 'sex goddess'!"

Stella swore under her breath and shoved the garment back on the rack. "This is ridiculous. I bloody hate shopping for undies, and for what?"

"If you want Dave to jump your bones, you need

to give him a good incentive." Jess raised her perfectly brushed brows and tittered. "When's he back?"

"Tonight, but he'll be buggered."

"You won't be sexing him up *any* night if you wear crap like that!"

Stella's shoulders sagged and she let out a sigh.

"Let's call it a day," Jess said. "I need a coffee."

Stella was all shopped-out and eagerly nodded her agreement. The pair made their way out of the store and headed off towards a coffee shop, but as they neared Gloria Jeans café, Jess came to a halt.

"Oh my God! This!" she said, pointing to a mannequin in the window of GiftMart, grabbing Stella's arm and leading her into the store.

"You've got to be kidding!" Stella said, her eyes wider than the Grand Canyon. "I am NOT wearing that!"

"Do you want a shag or not?" Jess pawed at the boxes lined up on a shelf next to the window. "Ah… here it is." She plucked one up and held it out.

"Nooo! And it'll never fit me, anyway."

"One size fits all," Jess said, reading the label then

eyeing Stella's mango-sized breasts.

Stella grimaced and ping-ponged between glaring at Jess and scrutinising the offending item.

"Has it really come to this?" she said, groaning.

"I think you know the answer to that," Jess replied and frog-marched Stella to the checkout.

Stella plopped her shopping bags on the kitchen counter and rifled through the contents. After putting away her groceries and laying out new undies for Poppy and socks and jocks for Dillon in their bedrooms, she made a cuppa and sat on the lounge with the bag containing *that* purchase, made on Jess's insistence. She pulled out the box and re-read the label.

Will this do the trick?

Stella shook her head and started to giggle like a schoolboy reading a porno mag. She'd never worn anything like this before, and although she wouldn't describe herself as a prude by any stretch of the imagination—her recent seduction attempts were testimony to her willingness to try anything—she would admit to being a missionary mistress when it came to romps in the bedroom. But she knew the time had come to up the ante higher than ever before, and with no further options forthcoming and her sex life still being as dried up as a billabong in high summer, she resigned herself to now trying *anything* to introduce some sweet seduction into her and Dave's marriage.

Stella finished her cuppa, made her way to the bedroom and began undressing. She opened the box and held out the contents, scrutinising and twisting them into shape. When she finally managed to put them on—a feat involving much contorting, swearing and readjusting—she stood in front of the mirror… and roared with laughter.

She laughed so much tears streamed down her cheeks, and she doubled-up as her sides ached.

Dave's gonna piss himself when he sees this!

Stella was waiting outside Poppy's classroom as Jess approached, a broad grin on her face.

"Well?" she said, eyebrows raised.

"Well what?"

"Did you try it on?"

"Uh-huh."

"And?"

Stella couldn't hold back and erupted into a fit of giggles.

"Oh my god, Jess. It took me twenty minutes just to get the damn thing on! And don't get me started on the coverage."

"I don't think coverage is the point of it," Jess said, snorting as she laughed.

"What are you two so happy about?" Nina joined the huddle.

"Well, you know how Stell's been trying to spice up her sex life… and it hasn't really gone to plan?"

"Sex life. Remind me what one of those is, again." Nina said, smirking.

"I'll let you know when I find out," Jess replied.

"So what's happening with Stell's sex life now?" Nina continued.

"Well, we found something on our shopping trip that should do the trick."

"We?" Stella said, snorting. "YOU found it, you mean."

"Oh…?" Nina said, leaning in closer.

"Dave will be in for a very sweet surprise," Jess said, grinning like the cat that got the *whole* jug of cream.

The three mums all fell about laughing just as the siren went and kids rushed out of classrooms, Poppy hurtling into her mum, wrapping her arms around Stella's neck.

"What are you laughing about, Mummy?"

"Nothing, Popsicle. Go play with Pearl while we wait for Dill."

With Poppy out of earshot, Stella beckoned Nina to huddle in.

"So, what I've bought will hopefully seal the deal with Dave when he gets back."

"Was it on the list?"

"Absolutely not!"

"Oh. Now I'm intrigued. Tell me more."

"Let's just say it'll satisfy Dave's sweet tooth," Stella said, chuckling.

"I don't know whether to be horrified or *jealous*," Nina said, winking.

When Dave arrived home, Stella had already

finalised her plan of attack: she would let him rest the next day—it always took him a good day or so to readjust—and would arrange for the kids to go to Jess's that night so her and Dave could have some quality alone time. She'd make sure he laid off the beer and would bombard him with "sexts" throughout the day to ramp up the heat in preparation for his 'treat'.

By the following lunchtime, all seemed to be going to plan and Stella hadn't once mentioned to Dave what she had in store for him. The 'sexting' seemed to be doing the trick; all indications were that Dave was indeed *up for it*.

With Poppy and Dillon dispatched to Jess's after school pickup, Stella drove home and set about organising dinner. Dave was lounging in the family room and catching up on the footy, so she prepped the ingredients for chicken in white wine, placed them all in a casserole dish and popped it in the oven to slow cook for a few hours, giving plenty of time for the starter she had in mind.

"When's dinner gonna be ready?" Dave's voice carried from the loungeroom. "It smells great."

"About seven," Stella said, tidying up the kitchen bench.

"But I'm hungry now."

"You'll just have to wait. Besides, I've got something that might just tide you over." A wry smile crossed her lips and she let out a chaste giggle.

Within seconds, Dave was behind her, wrapping his arms around her waist and nuzzling her ear. "Does this have anything to do with those text messages?"

"Maybe." Stella turned to face him. "Now, go wait on the sofa and I'll text you when your starter is ready."

Dave nestled into her neck. "Can't wait," he breathed.

Jeez—this might actually work!

Stella made her way to the bedroom and shut the door. She didn't want Dave to see her struggling to don the 'treat' she had for him.

When she'd finally untangled it all, put it on and rearranged it several times, she grabbed her phone and lay on the bed.

Are you ready? she texted Dave.

Dave was in the bedroom quicker than a greyhound chasing a rabbit and dispatched with his clothes in about the same amount of time, socks remaining, of course.

"Come to bed, honey," Stella purred, pulling the doona up around her in anticipation of the big reveal.

Dave launched himself onto the bed, yanked back the covers and stopped abruptly, hovering over her and gawping.

"And what do we have here?" he said, pawing at her new purchase.

"It's your starter… or should I say *dessert*."

"Is it edible?"

"Uh-huh. Fancy a nibble?"

Dave's eyes lit up like a halogen hob, and he licked his lips as he took in the sight of his wife wearing a candy bra and matching knickers held together with elastic string. He twanged a shoulder strap.

"I like candy," he said rasping, and nuzzled between Stella's breasts.

He took a nibble on one of the candies, but as he

did, the elastic stretched and pinged back on Stella's chest.

"Ow!" she yelled. "Go easy will you."

Dave let out a titter and looked up at his wife. "Where should I go next?" he said in a molten tone and trailed a finger from the centre of the bra down to the top of the knickers. But with the wry smile like that of a kid with a box of matches, he deliberately twanged a strap causing Stella to wince, and she instinctively swiped at his head.

It seemed to Stella that Dave was enjoying having his dessert served on a warm, soft plate, but she was getting the butt end of the deal. Perhaps she should have bought him a candy G-string to even the game, but then the image of pastel-coloured beads of sugary delight wedged in Dave's bum crack caused an involuntary gag.

Dave was oblivious to it all as he bit down, chomping and slurping as he went along. But every time he teased a candy off with his teeth, the strings tightened around Stella's torso and twanged against her skin causing her to yelp.

This is not quite the sexy time I had in mind.

Still, Stella was determined to fuel their love life, even if it meant taking a sugar-coated wedgie for the team.

Dave, ravenously filling up on Stella's appetisers, had bitten his way through a third of the bra, oblivious to the pain he was inflicting on his wife.

As he munched away, not only did the string almost cut off the circulation to her breasts, but the candy beads pressed into her flesh causing her to flinch involuntarily.

It all got too much for Stella and she pushed against Dave's face to get him to ease off, but as his head went back, his face reddened and he let out a sound akin to a cat throwing up a hairball, pumping his chest with his hand as dry coughing ensued.

"Dave?" Stella said, bolting upright. "Oh my God! Are you choking?"

Stella wriggled out from under him as he coughed and wheezed.

Dave tried to nod, mouthing, "water."

Stella leapt up from the bed and ran out of the bedroom to fetch a glass of water from the kitchen, hot-footing it all the way.

When she returned, Dave was writhing on the bed fighting for breath, his face crimson and eyes streaming.

"Drink Dave. Drink!" Stella yelled, her pulse racing and body shaking with fear. She thrust the water towards him and began slapping his back hoping to dislodge the offending candy bead but as she did, Dave grabbed the glass and glugged down the liquid splashing water all over the bed.

"Stop!" Dave croaked, shrugging off Stella's hand.

"I'll call the ambos!" she said, cupping her face as the brevity of the situation sank in. All she'd wanted was to inject some much-needed loving into their lives but had ended up almost killing Dave!

I thought sugar caused Diabetes not asphyxiation!

Dave took some more much-needed sips and his coughing abated, much to Stella's relief. He cleared his throat and paused for breath, blinking wildly.

"I don't need the ambos, just stop slapping me so damn hard."

"But it needs to come out!"

Dave took a deep breath then exhaled loudly. "I

think it's out."

"Are you sure? Let me check."

"Leave it, Stell. It's out!" Dave pushed her away and grimaced.

Stella perched on the bed, twisting the doona around her fingers as she struggled to think of what to say next.

"I'm hoping this wasn't what you had in mind as my sweet surprise," Dave finally said, growling.

"You got that right." Stella's eyes dropped, tears pricking the corners. "I just wanted us to have some long overdue fun." She slumped as her relief turned to despair.

"Is that what you call it."

"Don't be like that. I did it for us!" Stella's tears gave way to bubbling resentment and she pursed her lips, glaring at Dave.

And that's the last time I do!

Stella and Dave were at an impasse and in a fit of rage, Stella tugged at the candy bikini to yank it off, although to be fair, there wasn't much left of it. Cold, annoyed and resigned to the fact that any chance of a happy ending was futile, she huffed and whined as the threads finally gave way and the remaining beads fell onto the bed and across the floor.

"Hope you're gonna pick those up," Dave said, mumbling.

"I thought you'd want to eat them off the floor seeing as you're more interested in food than making love to your wife!" Stella's venom poured out as she stomped around the bedroom gathering up her clothes.

"What are you talking about? I thought this was meant to be fun."

"Well clearly it isn't. Maybe you shouldn't have tried to stuff so many of them in your mouth!"

"I wasn't stuffing them in my mouth. I thought it's what you wanted." Dave's face soured and he ran his hand through his hair. "Christ, there's no pleasing you, is there?"

"Pleasing me is easy, Dave. You just don't do it enough."

"What's that supposed to mean?"

"I'm the one who's tried to spice up our sex life *many* times. What have you done?"

"Nearly choked on a bloody lolly, that's what!"

Silence descended.

Stella glared at Dave.

Dave scowled at Stella.

"So that's it, then?" Dave said in a murmur.

"You got that right. That's the last time I try and tickle your fancy." Stella folded her arms in mock defiance.

"I guess a blow job's out of the question?"

"You have got to be kidding me—" With anger bubbling like a boiling kettle, Stella picked up a pillow and repeatedly whacked Dave with it.

"Ow, Stella. Give up will you!"

But there was no stopping her venom pouring out.

"You ungrateful, unworthy piece of—"

Before any more words could spill out, Dave had plucked up a pillow and was on the defensive, blocking Stella's onslaught, pillows bashing together again and again until feathers flitted and floated about them.

"Now look what you've done!" Stella barked.

"What *I've* done? You started it."

"Did I? Well, I guess I'll be the one to finish it

then, arsehole."

Stella swiped at Dave with the pillow once again, dislodging more feathers and causing Dave to curl up with his pillow covering his face.

"Stop being such a bitch!" he yelled.

"Well you stop being an ungrateful sod, then!" Stella fired back.

"Right that's it, you're gonna get it now!"

"Chance'd be a fine thing!" Stella was fuming, swiping at Dave left, right and centre, feathers now bursting out and floating like a blizzard around the bedroom.

Dave made one last-ditch attempt at an offensive blow but missed by miles and toppled backwards over the edge of the bed, thudding onto the bedroom floor.

Dave yelped.

Stella gasped, bolting upright.

"Dave? Are you okay?" she said, looking down at the dishevelled Dave now covered with a spattering of feather snow.

Before either could sling any more unsavoury comments or bash the pillows, smiles cracked both of their faces. Those smiles quickly became contagious chuckles, which led to full-blown belly-laughs.

Stella dropped to the floor, and it wasn't long before the pair of them were rolling about holding their stomachs as laughter gripped them and wouldn't let go.

When the laughter finally subsided and with a glint in his eye, Dave scooped Stella into his arms, whispering, "I do appreciate what you did for me, and I'm sorry it's been so long since we did anything like this." He kissed her forehead and traced a finger down her arm. "Just don't try to choke me next time, eh?"

Stella shivered, not from being cold but from that long yearned-for spark igniting and zooming all the way to her nether regions. She cupped a hand around Dave's face and pulled his lips to hers, sealing her desire with the brush of a kiss.

Dave moaned and pressed his lips hard against hers, and Stella realised he was no longer hungry for candy, but ravenous for the taste of her.

Dave pulled back a touch. "Is it too late for

dessert?" he said, rasping.

"Oh Dave," Stella cooed, "it's never too late for something sweet."

The following Monday at school pickup, Jess and Nina bounded up to Stella, eyebrows raised in an expectant gaze.

"Well?" they said in unison.

"Well what?" Stella said coyly.

"The candy bra and knickers–" Jess said with urgency. "Did they do the trick?"

Stella smiled.

"Maybe. I don't want to kiss and tell." She pressed a finger to her lips.

"Oh come on. Tell us!" Nina said, scowling.

"Did it work or not?" Jess said, frowning.

"Oh, it worked, just not in the way I'd planned."

"What's that supposed to mean?"

"Well, let's just say that Dave's on a sugar-free diet from now on."

The End

ABOUT THE AUTHOR

Lisa Wolstenholme is a multi-published author of contemporary women's fiction. She writes predominantly about life and loss, with a dash of love sometimes thrown in for good measure.

Lisa was previously on the board of management for the Katharine Susannah Prichard (KSP) Writers' Centre in WA and ran their member publishing service, Wild Weeds Press for many years.

She is now the director of Dragonfly Publishing, and, when not loitering around the Perth Hills, can be found writing stories where a main character usually dies, and drinking more SSB than is good for her.

Find out more about Lisa's authorship at:

www.lisawolstenholme.com.

ABOUT DRAGONFLY PUBLISHING

Dragonfly Publishing is a boutique publisher and publishing services company based in the beautiful Perth Hills in Western Australia.

Their aim is to ensure an author's publishing journey is enjoyable and transformative and pride themselves on their hand-holding ethos.

For more information, please see their website at:

www.dragonflypublishing.com.au

To contact Dragonfly Publishing, please email:

info@dragonflypublishing.com.au

9 780645 437058